EYES OF TERROR

BY

MRS. L. T. MEADE

British Library Cataloguing-in-Publication Data
A catalogue record for this book is available from
the British Library

Contents

MRS. L. T. MEADE

Elizabeth Thomasina Meade was born in County Cork, Ireland in 1844. She started writing speculative fiction at a very young age, which horrified her father, a Protestant clergyman. Upon the death of her mother, Meade moved to London, where she spent much time in the Reading Room of the British Museum. In 1879, she married Alfred Toulim Smith. Over the course of her life, Meade was a prolific author, producing more than 280 books and numerous short stories and articles for magazines such as *The Strand Magazine* and *Lady's Pictorial.* At her peak, she was publishing more than ten novels a year. She was best known for her female adventure novels, of which she penned more than thirty, but wrote in a number of genres, from romantic to detective fiction. Meade also co-edited *Atalanta,* a girl's magazine, and was an active feminist. She died in 1914.

EYES OF TERROR

by Mrs. L. T. Meade

~~~~~~

The strange story which I am about to tell happened just when the late war in South Africa was at its height. I was in a very nervous condition at the time, having lost my dear father, who was killed in action shortly before the taking of Pretoria. The news of my father's death reached us on a certain evening in May, just when the days were approaching their longest, and summer, with all its beauties, was about to visit the land. It was immediately afterwards that the visitations which I am about to describe took place. They were of a very alarming character, and so much did they upset my mental equilibrium that I determined to put my case into the hands of a certain Professor Ellicott, who was not only a physician and surgeon in the ordinary sense, but was also a man of great learning and keen original research.

I had met the Professor once at the house of a neighbour, and on that occasion had admired him, not only for his intellectual appearance, but also for the massive strength of his face and the calmness of his bearing. I knew that a strong man, who was also sympathetic and tactful, would not laugh at a girl's fears, however unreasonable he might consider them, and had not the least doubt that I should receive a patient hearing when I told him my story.

My name is Nora Dallas. I am twenty-one years of age. I have lived all my life in a beautiful old place about a mile and a half from the town of Ashingford. Professor Ellicott lived in the High Street, and I was fortunate enough to find him at home.

I sent in my card and was immediately admitted into his presence. He was a man of about thirty, with resolute grey eyes and a determined chin. He gave me a quick glance when I entered the room; then, without uttering a word, pointed to a chair.

"I am called Nora Dallas," I said.

"I know," he replied, in a gentle voice. "You are the daughter of that Colonel Dallas whose gallant action, when he sacrificed his life for his country on the march to Pretoria, is the talk and admiration of the country."

My eyes filled with tears.

"It is only three weeks since I heard of my father's death," I said. "You will forgive me sir, but I cannot bear any sympathetic reference to the subject, at least for the present."

"I understand," he replied, his hard face softening. "And now, what can I do for you?"

"I want to consult you as a doctor."

"But I am not a consultant—I mean that I do not practise medicine in the ordinary sense."

"I am aware of that fact," I answered. "And just for that very reason, Professor Ellicott, I have been compelled to come to you."

"I do not quite understand."

He looked at me with the dawn of a smile on his lips.

"I think you will give me a frank opinion, and be unbiased by the red-tapism which causes many medical men to hide the truth from their patients."

"Ah, you think well of me," he said, with a smile, "and I perceive that you are a brave woman. Nevertheless, I must inform you that I am scarcely qualified to enter into your case. My work lies altogether in the regions of original research."

"May I at least tell you my story?" I insisted. "You can make up your mind afterwards whether you will help me or not."

His reply to this was to get up and pace the room, stopping once or twice to look at me, then continuing his slow, measured tread up and down. I did not interrupt him. I sat as still as though carved in marble.

"You must forgive my apparent rudeness, Miss Dallas," he said, "but I was endeavouring to recall what I had already heard about you. I remember everything now. I met you a month ago at Sir John Newcome's. You live at Courtlands, one of the finest places in the neighbourhood. You are an only child. Doubtless, now that your father is dead, you are wealthy. You have lived at Courtlands almost all your life. Of course, Miss Dallas, you have your own family physician?"

"Yes," I answered.

"Will you not consult him?"

"No; for he is not the man for my purpose."

He smiled.

"You think that I am?"

"If anyone can help me, you can."

"How like a woman!" he said, somewhat impatiently. "And yet you know nothing about me. As I said just now, I am not a consultant. I have come to Ashingford for quiet, and for the opportunity to examine into the length and breadth of a problem which, if I can bring it to a successful issue, will mean health and happiness to millions. And yet a girl, little more than a child, wants to interrupt my train of thought. Do you think you are fair to me?"

"I don't know anything about that," I replied, with vehemence. "I only know that I want help. Will you give it to me?"

My voice broke.

"Of course I will," he said, cordially, and his whole manner completely altered. "I only said what I did to test you. Now we will preamble no more. Tell me your story."

"I was twenty-one last March," I began, immediately, "and now that my dear father is dead I am absolutely my own mistress. With the exception of my Aunt Sophia, my father's sister, who lives with me, and my two cousins, I am without relations. It is about these cousins that I wish specially to speak. They are the sons of my father's younger brother, who has long been dead. My father adopted them in their infancy, brought them up, sent them to school, and gave them all they required. They are twins and are now five-and twenty years of age. Rudolf has been called to the Bar and Lionel is a solicitor. Professor Ellicott, I must be truthful—I must be truthful even at the risk of failing in charity. My cousins are not good men. I have nothing to say against them—I have no means at present of proving my words—nevertheless, instinct tells me that I am right. Rudolf is the sort of man who imposes on people. I have seen him rhapsodize over poetry or a sunset, and his friends then imagine that he has a great love for the beautiful. But I know better. The only love in his wicked heart is the love of money. Lionel is his weak shadow—his dupe and tool."

"Surely you are hard on your cousins?"

"You would naturally think so; and yet I hope to convince you that I have read their characters aright.

"My father, before he went to South Africa, made a will, the contents of which he fully explained to me. In the event of his death I was to inherit the house and estate and also the bulk of his money, with the exception of a sum of sixty thousand pounds, which was to be divided between my two cousins. He fully explained all that he wanted to tell me with regard to his last will, and gave me directions as to certain affairs which he wished to be specially attended to. My dear father then continued to say some words which astonished and distressed me very much. He declared that it was the darling wish of his heart that Rudolf and I should marry. My father said that he had the highest opinion of my cousin and assured me that nothing would make him happier than such a marriage. Rudolf had told him of his attachment to me—an attachment which I knew well did not exist.

"I heard my father in silence. Then I gave an emphatic negative to the whole proposal. My father listened in amazement. I said that I neither liked nor trusted my cousin, and that nothing—no words, no conditions—would make me accept him. After a pause my father said that my feelings must be my guide, but he continued:

" 'I cannot agree with your opinion, and I sincerely hope that time may alter it.'

"From the hour of his depature there began for me a detestable period, during which I was persecuted by Rudolf's odious attentions. As he and Lionel practically lived in our house, you can imagine that it was impossible for me to escape altogether from his presence. But at last it became so intolerable that I wrote to my father on the subject. I told Rudolf quite frankly that I was doing so, and even made him acquainted with the greater part of my letter. In that letter I told my father that he did not rightly gauge his nephew's character, that he was not what he believed him to be, and, in order to prove my words, I mentioned a few instances which, unconvincing to a stranger like yourself, might have the effect of opening his eyes.

"That letter was posted two months ago. Up to the present I have had no reply to it, but am even now waiting and hoping to hear my father's views on the subject. Important letters must be on the road from South Africa for me. I have only received the news of my dear father's death by cablegram."

My voice broke. I paused, struggling with emotion; then I continued:

"I am sorry to trouble you, Professor Ellicott, with this long preamble. I am now approaching that strange thing about which I wish to consult you.

"We received the cablegram acquainting us with the news of my father's death on a certain morning towards the end of last month. On the evening of that same day another long cablegram from South Africa was put into Rudolf's hands. He was sitting with my aunt and me in the drawing-room when he received it. He opened it, was evidently very much upset, but refused to divulge its contents. He called Lionel to his side, and they left the room together. I saw them pacing up and down in the shrubbery, evidently consulting with regard to the contents of the cablegram, but never from that hour till now have I heard the slightest inkling of what it was about.

"Three days later my father's will was read and my cousins heard of the large sums of money which would fall to their share. They fully expected to be remembered in my father's will, but not to such a generous extent, and their satisfaction was very great. As to Rudolf, his face quite beamed with delight, and they were both in feverish haste to possess themselves of the money. Mr. Brewster, our family lawyer, however, said that it would be impossible for them to receive their legacies for several weeks, as probate would have to be taken and other preliminaries attended to. Finally he made the remark:

"Nothing can really be done until Colonel Dallas's letters and papers arrive from South Africa. This can scarcely be expected until a month from the present date.'

"On that very evening my elder cousin came to me again and once more implored me to become his wife. He spoke of my father and his well-known wishes on the subject, and pleaded with such power that had I not known him well I might have been touched into a semblance of kindness by his manner. I did know my cousin, however, and told him so in unmistakable terms. He seemed to struggle with emotion for a minute; then he said, rising as he spoke:

" 'All right, Nora, I see I must accept your verdict. You may be sure that I will not trouble you on this subject again. It would be brutal to do so," he added, "for you are looking very ill. I see it in your eyes. '

" 'I am not exactly ill,' I answered. 'I am naturally in very great trouble, but I am no more really ill than you are.'

" 'I am all right, ' he said, with a shrug of his shoulders. 'But your nerves, poor Nora, are in a sad condition. You have received a most serious shock, and it is telling on you. You ought to be exceedingly careful. I mean it is your duty to be much more careful than most women. '

" 'I don't understand you,' I answered. 'And I wish,' I added, 'that you would leave me now.'

" 'I will in a minute,' he said, and then he approached quite close to my side.

" 'One word before I go,' he went on, and he fixed his great, strong, dark eyes on mine. 'Whether you like me or whether you hate me we are cousins, Nora. Our family history is well known to each of us. I in particular, however, have studied medicine, and am therefore in a position to speak. I only gave up medicine for the Bar because I thought I saw a more speedy way of earning money in that profession. Now, Nora, listen. Raise your eyes to mine. Don't shrink, child. If you encourage the morbid fancies which are now filling your brain you will share the fate of poor Aunt Ethel. I know what I am talking about. The pupils of your eyes point to a disordered brain.'

"He left me. I sat still for a minute, feeling more nervous and disturbed than I cared to own. Then I went to Aunt Sophia.

" 'What is the matter, Nora?' she said, when I found her. 'You are trembling all over and looking so ill. What is wrong child?'

" 'I want to ask you a straight question,' I replied. 'Who was, or who is, Aunt Ethel? I have never heard of her.'

"Aunt Sophia looked startled. She did not speak for a minute; then she said, with considerable reluctance:

" 'It doesn't matter about your Aunt Ethel. She has been long in her grave. Let her memory rest in peace.'

" 'But what about her?' I said. 'I *will* know,' I continued, and then I repeated what Rudolf had told me.

"Aunt Sophia looked very queer. After a futher pause she said:

" 'Rudolf has done wrong, but as you know so much you may as well know all. Your Aunt Ethel was your father's eldest sister. She went mad when about your age, and eventually ended her days by suicide.'

" 'And I was never told,' I said, turning white.

" 'Why should you be told?'

" 'But there must be insanity in our family.'

" 'Hers was the only case. Don't think about it again, child. Busy yourself with those active employments which a woman in your position has naturally so much to do with.'

"I left Aunt Sophia and returned to my room. There was a moon in the sky. My bedroom windows were open. I lit a pair of candles at each side of the long mirror at one end of the room, and deliberately studied my face. I had always known that my eyes were somewhat peculiar, my pupils being more dilated than those of most women."

"That fact merely betokens a high degree of nervous sensibility," said the Professor.

"I examined my eyes that night," I continued, "and it did seem to me that they had a wild and startled glance. I called my courage to my aid, however, and determined not to be fanciful, and to try to forget my cousin's words. That was easily said, but very difficult to act upon. My courage certainly did ebb as night went on. I found that my thoughts dwelt on Aunt Ethel and her horrible fate, and also found that I could turn them in no other direction. Presently I went to the window and looked out into the beautiful night. The moonlight was falling across the grass and causing black shadows under the trees.

"Suddenly I uttered a scream and fell back, too startled to keep my self-control. For gazing at me fixedly out of the deep mass of foliage were two very bright, luminous eyes, eyes full of a strange and terrifying gleam. I saw them as distinctly as I now see you. I watched them move, and saw them glitter as they disappeared into the darkness. When they had quite vanished I knew that I was cold all over. I shivered with a most awful sense of dread. My first desire was to run straight to Aunt Sophia, tell her the whole truth, and beg of her to share my room for the night. But on reflection I resolved not to do this. I did not want Aunt Sophia to know. She would certainly not have believed my tale, and she would put down the vision which I had seen to the same cause of which Rudolf would doubtless attribute it.

"There was no repose for me that night. The thought of those eyes kept me company—the eyes themselves and Rudolf's significant words: 'If you encourage those morbid fancies you will share the fate of poor Aunt Ethel. The pupils of your eyes point to a disordered brain.'

"In the afternoon of the next day I went for a solitary walk by myself. We have pine woods at the back of our house. From there I could see at intervals the tower which is the oldest part of the mansion. It is situated at the end of a long, rambling building, and was in existence at least four centuries ago. It is a curious Old Norman tower, with arches over the windows and a castellated roof. The tower contains only two rooms, the lower one being the library of our house and the upper my father's study. Since his death no one has been near that part of the building. I felt a sense of reproach as I remembered his room now. Was his study neglected and covered with dust? Were the flowers in the vases dried up and dead? I would go to the study tomorrow and see that it was made fresh and clean. I would open the windows and let in the sweet air. Nay, more, when the long-looked-for and eagerly expected letters arrived from South Africa I would read them in my father's study.

"That evening I paced up and down for a long time in the pine

woods, then I returned to the house. I took up a novel and tried to
read, but the book did not suit my mood. I remembered another
which had begun to interest me, and which I had left in one of the
drawing-rooms. I went downstairs to fetch it. There was no one in
the room. I found the book in a distant corner and returned slowly to
my bedroom. To do this I had to go down a long corridor into which
many opened. For some extraordinary reason the electric light in
this corridor was not turned on. I noticed how dark it was, and just
as I reached my own door I looked back, impelled, I suppose, by
instinct. In the darkness at the father end of the corridor I again saw
the gleaming eyes. They stared fixedly at me without blinking, and
with a horrible leering expression in their gaze. Again I screamed,
rushed into my room, and locked the door. I could scarcely endure
my misery.

" 'Am I going mad or am I the victim of an apparition?' I said to
myself. 'Is my brain giving way? What am I to do? How am I to
endure this? How am I to live?'

"The next week or ten days passed without any futher disturbance,
and I was beginning to recover my mental balance. Rudolf was away
from home during the greater part of that time, engaged on some
very special business in the North of England. I was undoubtedly
happier and less nervous when he was absent, but when he returned
his affectionate and concerned manner about me made me self-
reproachful, and I almost wondered at myself for the intolerable
feeling of repugnance which I always felt towards him.

"Two or three nights after his return I saw the eyes again. On this
occasion they stared at me from the centre of the rose-lawn. The
night was black as pitch, and there were the eyes raised between
five and six feet above the ground, and staring full at me with
unblinking directness. After this visitation I determined to see you
at once. Now, can you help me? Have I been visited by an apparition
or am I mad? Tell me what you really think."

For reply the Professor said, quietly:

"I will examine your own eyes before I pronounce an opinion."

I rose at once. He placed me in a chair in front of a large window
and, taking up some powerful lenses, carefully looked into both my
eyes. When the examination was over he said:—

"You are very nervous. Some of the higher nerve centres are in a state of irritation. Your Father's death, joined to the shock of this apparition, trick, or what you like to call it, has been too much for you. You ought really to leave home."

"But am I going mad?"

"There is no trace of a disordered brain. Nevertheless you are nervous, and nerves are kittle cattle, and ought to be attended to."

"But, Dr. Ellicott, why should I be nervous? Why should I see those ghastly eyes? What is the mystery?"

"I should like much to unravel it," he said, with a shrug of his shoulders.

"How I wish you would!"

He looked thoughtful for a minute or two; then he said:

"Would it be possible for you to invite me to stay at Courtlands?"

"Would you come?"

"Could you give me a room where I could continue my business without interruption?"

"I could hand you over the library in the old tower. There you need never hear a footfall, for the tower is at the end of an unused wing at a remote part of the building."

"In that case I will bring my things and spend a few days at Courtlands. I do not believe in your apparition as an apparition, nor do I think that you are becoming insane. Your case interests me. May I arrive in time for dinner this evening?"

"I don't know how to thank you," was my answer.

"Expect me at Courtlands about seven o'clock. And now leave me, like a good girl, for I have many things to attend to."

I returned home with a great sense of relief, just in time for lunch. The only people at table were Aunt Sophia and my Cousin Lionel.

"Why, Nora," cried my aunt, "how much better you look! Have you had good news?"

"Yes and no," I replied. "By the way, Aunt Sophy, can we entertain a visitor for the next few days?"

"A visitor now?" she said, raising her brows in astonishment.

Lionel laid down his knife and fork and looked hard at me.

"To receive a visitor in the house now would be unusual, would it not, Nora?" he said, gently. "My uncle has not been dead a month yet."

I took no notice of him, but turned again to Aunt Sophia.

"Dr. Ellicott, the well-known Professor, is staying at Ashingford," I said. "I met him some time ago at the Newcomes'. He is a remarkably clever man, and I may as well confess that I consulted him medically this morning. No more Dr. Jessops for me. I preferred to consult one who was well up-to-date on medical matters. The Professor interests me and I interest him. He wishes to come here for a few days in order to watch my symptoms. He will arrive in time for dinner. Please, Aunt Sophy, will you order the green room to be got ready for him, and also the library in the old tower?"

I spoke in a decided manner, and neither my aunt nor Lionel ventured to remonstrate, for, after all, I was really mistress.

Suddenly I turned to my cousin.

"Is Rudolf away again?" I asked.

"No," he replied; "Rudolf is unwell. His eyes are hurting him. He is obliged to stay in a darkened room."

"I did not know that Rudolf suffered from his eyes."

"He never did until lately. We neither of us can imagine what is the matter with them," was Lionel's response.

I said a word or two of commonplace condolence, and then left the room.

That evening the Professor arrived, and when I entered the drawing-room before dinner I noticed that my aunt and both my cousins were waiting to receive him. During dinner he made himself generally agreeable, and Rudolf in especial seemed to be attracted by his manner and powers of conversation. I noticed, however, rather to my amazement, that my elder cousin wore a shade over his eyes, and in the course of dinner I inquired what really ailed them.

"I don't know," he said. "I am in considerable pain. My eyes are very much inflamed."

"Will you permit me to do something to relieve your symptoms?" said Professor Ellicott, suddenly, turning as he spoke, raising his pince-nez, and fixing his gaze on Rudolf's face.

"I wish you would," was the reply.

"I will look at your eyes after dinner. And now, Miss Dallas," he continued, turning with courtesy to my aunt, "let me explain that knotty point to you."

He was discussing a little matter with regard to the growth of ferns, and Aunt Sophia, a keen botanist, was listening to him with rapt attention.

By-and-by I made the signal to leave the room, and the gentlemen were left to themselves. In the course of that same evening the Professor came to sit near me.

"I have examined your cousin's eyes. There is considerable inflammation both in the eyelids and the eyes themselves. Their condition points to a strange diagnosis, but as it seems impossible that it can be the right one I am not prepared to say anything further on the subject—at least now. Tell me are you going to have a good sleep tonight?"

"I hope so."

"I think you will, for I have prepared a small, but effectual, draught, which I want you to take just as you are lying down. Get your maid to sleep in your room, and believe me that, eyes or no eyes, you will be in a state of oblivion five minutes after you take my draught."

I smiled, with a sense of relief.

"I believe," I said, "that in any case I should sleep well with you in the house."

The next few days passed without anything fresh occurring. We saw but little of the Professor. He was absorbed with his own work in the old library in the tower.

At last the day arrived when we expected letters and news from the beloved dead. Even Aunt Sophia was agitated, and Lionel and Rudolf were like restless ghosts, hovering here, there and everywhere. Rudolf's eyes looked worse than ever, and he also complained of a strange sore at his side. At dinner that evening the Professor said, abruptly:

"By the way, Dallas, do you happen to know anything about that new substance—radium?"

"I have heard of it," was the reply.

Lionel's face became suddenly rigid and very pale. Rudolf, on the contrary, looked with the utmost composure at Professor Ellicott.

"You, of course, have studied its properties," he said. "Tell me about them. I dabble in many things, and, above all enjoyments, to peer into the mysteries of science delights me most. But give me an account of the properties of radium."

14

"They are too varied to mention here. I will but allude to one or two. In close contact with the skin, radium has the effect of absolutely destroying the epidermis and the true skin beneath, thus in time producing an open sore. Moreover," said the Professor, "were you really dabbling with this strange substance the state of your eyes would be accounted for."

"I have never even seen the thing," was the abrupt answer.

The conversation turned to other matters. After dinner we all went to the drawing-room. Professor Ellicott came and seated himself near me.

"You will receive a letter from your father by the next post?" he asked.

"Yes."

"Where will you read it?"

"In his study. I have always read his letters there. I made him a promise that I would do so. He said he would like to think of me sitting under my mother's portrait, reading his letters and thinking of him."

A few minutes afterwards the postman's ring was heard, and a servant entered with several letters on a salver. The one I had expected was handed to me, and there was also a foreign letter for Aunt Sophia. Rudolf, who had come into the room just before the servant brought the letters, came up to me.

"You will go away by yourself and read your letter," he said, kindly. "You will read it in your father's study, won't you?"

I nodded. He smiled.

"I felt sure you would go there, Nora. He will be with you in spirit."

As Rudolf uttered the last words he glanced towards Lionel, and the two left the room a minute or two before I did.

To reach the tower I had to go down a long corridor which was seldom used. At the farther end of the corridor was a baize door which opened on to some narrow stone stairs. They were worn with age. Mounting them, I soon reached my father's study on the top floor of the tower. It was octagonal in shape, with many windows. These windows were closely barred and the panes of glass were small. When I entered the room I gave a start of surprise. I expected to see it in darkness, but instead of that a small table had been

P

drawn up within a foot or two of the high, old-fashioned grate, and on it were placed a pair of brass candlesticks with candles in them already lighted. But why were the blinds not drawn down at the windows? I felt a momentary inclination to repair this omission myself, but my father's letter occupied all my thoughts and I soon forgot everything but the fact that I was about to read the beloved words—in short, to receive a message from the dead.

The contents of my father's letter absorbed my complete attention, and I soon perceived that only the very early portion was written by himself; most of it had evidently been dictated to a certain Edward Vincent, whose name, as one of the young lieutenants in my father's regiment, was already familiar to me. The letter told me that my father was mortally wounded, and that he was now partly writing, partly dictating his last good-bye to me in the tent where they had removed him after the skirmish with the enemy. In the letter he told me that he had received my last communication, and, in consequence, had made inquiries, which took some little time to come to fruition. On that very morning, however, he had received a long letter from London, which contained a complete confirmation of what I had told him, and also many other revelations had been forthcoming, which filled him with the utmost displeasure and horror. He therefore resolved immediately to change his will, leaving none of his property to my cousins, but all to me. The last words of his letter desired me to turn to the opposite page, on which a formally-worded will was written. This will left everything to me. I turned to it and read it. It was very short, and was signed by my father, and had also the signatures of two witnesses.

Tears flowed from my eyes. In one sense I was relieved, and yet my heart was torn. I covered my face. Just then a slight noise, which might have been attributed to the tapping of a bough against the window-pane, caused me to turn my head. I did so tremblingly. I felt convinced that I was not alone. Something, or someone, was looking at me. Fascinated, I gazed straight before me. Again came that ghastly tap, which I felt sure, proceeded from no human hand. I looked towards the upper panes of one of the windows, and there were the eyes. Never had they seemed more malicious or horrible. I lost my nerve, gave one shrill and terrified scream, and rushed towards the door, altogether forgetting my letter, which lay upon the table.

I had just reached the door when a fresh thing happened. The room became full of a sudden and terrible wind. It caught at the table-cloth, flapping it violently. The letter, written on thin foreign paper and consequently light as air, floated off the table with one or two other loose letters, was carried straight to the fireplace, and then up the chimney. The next instant I felt my dress dragged as by an unseen power. Something seemed to draw me back into the room, and the candles on the table flickered and went out. I was in the dark and alone, yet not alone. What awful thing had happened? My brain swam for a minute. I felt sick and cold; then I lost consciousness.

When I returned to my senses I was lying on the sofa and Professor Ellicott was bending over me.

"Now, control yourself, Miss Dallas," he said. "We have not a moment to lose. Tell me exactly what occurred."

I pressed my hand to my face. There was a light again in the room.

"Be quick," said the Professor. "What did you see? Why did you cry out? I was coming into the house in a hurry—in fact, I was on my way to this room—when I heard your shriek. I had been smoking and walking up and down in the grounds. Something induced me to look towards the tower. All of a sudden I saw—but tell me first what did you see?"

"The eyes," I answered. "They looked at me through one of the windows—that one exactly facing the table."

"Through what part of the window did they look?"

"Through one of the topmost panes."

"Good! I thought so. Now go on. Tell me the rest."

"I lost my nerve. I rushed towards the door, and just as I got there I turned, for the room was full of wind."

"Wind!" said the Professor. "Why, the night is as calm as death."

"Nevertheless, the room was full of a sort of gale, and the letter—my father's letter—was lifted and carried towards the chimney, up which it disappeared, and I myself was dragged back into the room. Then the candles were put out. Oh, I do believe at last in the ghost. Professor Ellicott, I wish I were dead."

"Don't be so silly, child. I assure you there is no ghost. Now, listen. I also saw something."

"The eyes?"

He nodded.

"They flashed at me for an instant. I fancy, Miss Dallas, this is a very tangible ghost. I saw a figure crouching on the roof, bending down over the turret towards that very window. I was just under the tower, hastening in, when you screamed, and I looked up and saw it disappear behind the parapet. The eyes were visible for about half a second. We shall catch your ghost, don't be afraid, and solve your mystery. I shall remain here for the present, but we must have the roof examined, and at once. Do you know of any other way to get to it except by a ladder from the ground? There surely must be a trap–door somewhere."

"There is, " I answered, "There's a trap–door at the end of this very wing."

"Good!" said the Professor. "Go downstairs at once and get several men, your cousins amongst them, to examine the roof from end to end, and in especial to look on the roof of this tower. I will stay here. Don't be long."

I ran away. The Professor's words had excited me, and my courage had returned. I gave the alarm. I could not find my cousins, but soon the rest of the house was in a state of ferment. Some of the men–servants and two of the gardeners immediately ascended to the roof. They carefully examined not only the roof of the house, but that of the tower. But look as they would they could not see a single trace of any individual hiding there. It is true that a rope, fastened to one of the chimneys, was hanging close to one of the parapets of the tower. This alone pointed conclusively to the fact that someone had been there. Nothing else, however, was to be discovered.

Accompanied by Aunt Sophia I returned to the Professor.

"Four of our men have been on the roof," I said, "and they brought away this rope. You can see it, There was no one there."

"Ah!" He shrugged his shoulders. "I thought there must have been a rope. He could not have bent over so far without being secured against the possibility of falling."

"The rope was fastened round one of the chimneys," I continued.

"Profesor, what does this mean?" said poor Aunt Sophia.

"Where are your nephews, madam?" was his answer. "Why are they not helping in this search?"

"We cannot find my cousins anywhere," I answered. "The last I saw of them was when I was going upstairs to read my father's letter. They then left the drawing-room and went out of the house arm-in-arm."

"I will go and have a further search made for them," said my aunt. "They certainly ought to be acquainted with this most remarkable occurrence."

She gave me a suspicious and, I fancied, unbelieving glance. Did she really think that I was imagining the whole thing? The Professor's attitude, however, comforted me.

"Don't be alarmed, child," he said. "The clue which we seek is close at hand. I am convinced of it. Now we must do something. I shall remain in this room for the night, and one or two of the servants must watch on the roof of the tower. But you must go to bed and rest, otherwise you will be down with nervous fever. Now, tell me, please, Miss Dallas, who are the most trustworthy and absolutely reliable servants in your house?"

"Harris, the old gardener, for one," I answered. "He has been with us since before I was born."

"Who else?"

"Franks, the butler."

"Then Harris and Franks shall watch on the roof of the tower tonight. Now go to bed."

Against my will I was forced to go to my room. Another sleeping-draught, administered by the Professor, ensured my repose, and in the morning I was sufficiently calm even to defy Aunt Sophia's looks of suspicion, for suspect me now of incipient insanity she evidently did.

The mysterious disappearance of both my cousins caused a great deal of talk and speculation on the following morning, and I went to the tower to visit the Professor in a state of great excitement on the subject. His manners were absolutely non-committal. He refused to say anything about my cousins, and he also refused to leave the study.

"When I go someone else must take my place," he said. "This room must not be left unguarded for a single moment, nor must the roof above."

Towards the latter part of the day he suggested that I should take his place in the study while he himself examined the roof. In about half an hour he returned to me. I saw that he held a tiny glass tube in his hand.

"Can you make anything of this?" he said, laying it on the table before me.

"Nothing," I answered. "What is it?"

"A very valuable piece of evidence, I take it."

"What do you mean?"

"I will try to tell you. I found this tube in the gutter just above the window. It is, as you see, sealed up at each end. It looks innocent enough; nevertheless, it contains a very minute portion of that new substance—radium. You heard what I said to your Cousin Rudolf with regard to the effect of radium on the human skin, but I did not tell him that it does something else. When held for a short time in front of the eyes, the eyes take to themselves a certain amount of its properties, and they glow in the dark with a great luminosity which gives them a most terrifying appearance. It strikes me, Miss Dallas, that in this little bottle I hold the solution of your ghost. The eyes of a man who held radium a short distance from his pupils would also become very much inflamed. Consider the condition of your Cousin Rudolf's eyes. I found this tube in the gutter. We are getting near the clue; eh, don't you think so?"

I felt myself turning pale. I know that I trembled.

"Could any man living be so wicked?" was my next remark.

"Men will do strange things for money," was his answer. "But how your cousin would know that your father intended to change his will is a mystery which I cannot fathom."

"What do you mean to do next?" I asked.

"Watch for the scoundrels. They are hiding somewhere, and all in good time they will reappear. By the way, you say that your father's letter, containing the will, was blown up the chimney. James," he continued, turning to the servant who had just entered the room, "you and Andrews must come up here within an hour and take my place while I visit the roof. I may have to remain there for some hours this evening. Meanwhile, Miss Dallas," he continued, giving me a quick smile, "you shall go and take a constitutional."

I did not want to go out, but the Professor's word just then was my law. The evening was a lovely one, and I walked for some little time. As I returned I looked towards the tower. Suddenly I perceived the tall figure of the Professor. He was standing absolutely motionless near one of the chimneys. He evidently saw me, but did not make the slightest movement. A wild desire to be with him and to share his watch came over me. Quick as thought I entered the house, reached the trap-door, which was open, and soon was standing on the low roof of Courtlands. I walked warily and presently reached the edge of the parapet. There were two steps here leading from the roof of the house to the roof of the tower. I mounted them and stood by the Professor's side.

"Child," he said, in a whisper, "what are you doing?"

"I must share your watch," I said.

"I would rather be alone."

I shook my head.

"Something forces me to remain with you. Don't deny me my wish."

He held up his hand with a warning gesture to me.

"Then you must crouch by this parapet," he said, "and remain motionless. I shall hide behind the chimney. My suspicions are confirmed. There are men not far from here. I heard a movement not along ago. Absolute quiet will force the scoundrels from their lair."

I now perceived that he carried a revolver. Moving away from him a few paces I crouched down behind the parapet. He did likewise a little way off. We were the only watchers on the silent tower, but I knew that there were servants also on guard in the room below.

By-and-by the sun sank towards the west and twilight reigned over the scene. Twilight deepened into night.

The Professor and I had remained motionless, as though we were dead, for from two to three hours.

All of a sudden I saw Professor Ellicot raise himself and glance towards me. I could but dimly see his face, but I knew that something was about to happen. The next minute, peering hard towards the stack of chimneys, I noticed, to my unbounded horror, the head of my Cousin Rudolf show itself. He did not see us, and cautiously began to descend from the chimney on to the roof. Just as he was about to place his feet on the roof, Professor Ellicott, strong as steel, sprang upon him and dragged him by the shoulders and arms down upon his knees.

"I have been waiting for you," he said. As he spoke he held his revolver to my cousin's ear. "If you stir you are a dead man. Confess your crime at once. Your game is up! Now, then, what does this mean?"

Rudolf groaned.

"The agony in my eyes is past bearing," he said.

"Call to your brother to come out of his hiding-place. I will take you both to the Colonel's study. There you shall explain your villainies."

"Let me rise, and I promise you I will not try to escape," answered Rudolf. "I am in such pain that I am past caring for anything but the chance of relief. I will shout to Lionel. We have been starving and have been in the dark. Oh, the agony in my eyes!"

The Professor allowed Rudolf to rise. He went to the chimney and called down. In a moment Lionel made his appearance. Professor Ellicott then escorted the two men across the roof, down through the trap-door, and back again to my father's study.

"I cannot face the light," said Rudolf at once, covering his eyes with his hands. "I have endured more than I bargained for. If I am happy enough to escape without the punishment of the law, I will confess everything."

"That remains with Miss Dallas, for she is the person you have injured," said the Professor.

"Tell the truth, Rudolf. I won't be too hard on you," I answered, my voice trembling. I saw him shiver slightly. His tall, athletic figure was bowed. He still kept his face covered with his hand. As to Lionel, he was crouching in the attitude of an unmistakable cur in a distant corner.

"This is the story," said Rudolf. "There is no use any longer hiding things. I was in serious money trouble—Stock Exchange debts, the usual thing. The money left to me in my uncle's will would, however, have put me again on my feet. Were it for any reason withdrawn, nothing remained for me but open disgrace and ruin.

22

"For years it has been my one effort to keep my transgressions from my uncle's ears, and only for the extraordinary instinct which you, Nora, possessed, and which caused you to watch me as a cat watches a mouse, I should have succeeded in securing the fortune which he meant to leave me. Lionel was much in the same boat. We decided, therefore, to act together. For a long time we have been in league with a certain Lieutenant Vincent, a young officer in the same regiment as my uncle. My uncle was much attached to Vincent. In the hour of his death Vincent happened to be near, and it was to him my uncle dictated his letter, the letter which you received last night. On the afternoon of the day when the news of my uncle's death was received here I had a long cablegram from Vincent, in which he gave me briefly the contents of the new will, which was already on its way to England, and also said that both the witnesses, privates in my uncle's regiment, had been shot dead shortly after he breathed his last. Thus there were no witnesses to prove this will. He said we must make the best of his information, and we had a month to mature our plans in. We put our heads together and resolved on a course of action. We knew the history of Aunt Ethel. Nora has always had very highly strung nerves, and we perceived to our satisfaction that they were terribly upset by her father's death. I had been reading a good deal about the newly discovered substance —radium, and thought it possible that it might serve my purpose. I purchased a minute portion and began at once to work on my cousin's fears. Radium, as you know, when held near the eyes, can give them a luminous and very ghastly appearance. I got Nora to believe that she was the victim of a terrifying disorder, and you are aware how successfully my purpose worked. I further arranged, with Lionel's help, to deprive Nora of the fresh will as soon as she had read it; our belief being that her story would not be credited, and that when she spoke of a new will having been sent to her the whole thing, in combination with her story of the ghostly eyes, would be put down to insanity.

"Now, this was our plan: We knew that her habit was to read all letters received from her father in his study. We investigated this room thoroughly and made an important discovery. A few feet up the wide chimney was a secret chamber. The entrance to this chamber was approached by climbing down the inside of the chimney from the roof. This mode of entrance was facilitated by projecting bricks left for the purpose. We resolved to utilise the chamber for our requirements.

"As soon, therefore, as the post arrived from South Africa, Lionel and I left the drawing-room. We immediately went by the trap-door on to the roof. Lionel disappeared down the chimney into the secret chamber, where we had previously taken an immensely powerful exhaust-pump. In the bottom of the chimney there was placed a short time ago a large register, thus closing up the space except for a small hole in the centre, in order to let the smoke pass up. Leading from the exhaust-pump we had arranged a large tube, the mouth of which fitted exactly into the hole in the register. We had also put in order a small electric bell which communicated from the roof to the chamber. After Lionel had disappeared down the chimney I prepared my eyes, and at the right moment bent over the parapet.

"All the time Nora was reading her letter I was looking at her, and when I perceived that she had quite taken in its contents I attracted her attention by gently tapping on the window with a spray of ivy. She turned instinctively. Again I tapped, and she looked up and saw me. As my brother and I guessed she would, she uttered a scream and immediately tried to leave the room, forgetting the letter, which still lay on the table. I immediately rang the bell. Nora was too terrified to hear it. At the signal Lionel began to work the exhaust-pump by means of a hand wheel. It sucked the air out of the study, and drew the letter and other small papers up the chimney right into the tube. Thus we secured the letter and the new will.

"I then joined Lionel in the secret room, not forgetting to take with me the wires from the electric bell. We both immediately set to work to draw back the tube into the secret chamber, and by the time Nora had recovered consciousness all trace of our plot had virtually disappeared."

"What about the will? Have you destroyed it?" said the Professor.

"Strange to say, we have not," replied Lionel. "The fact is, we were in the dark and starving. We had hoped, but for your interference to get away in a few minutes. We have been incarcerated for twenty-four hours. Rudolf was in agony with his eyes. We wanted to read the will before tearing it up."

"Then you can give it to me?"

"Yes. We have it here intact, and, if our cousin will permit us, we will leave the country tomorrow and never trouble her again."

They did so. I did not wish to pursue them, as I doubtless could, with the punishment of the law. My terrors were over. Never more would the ghastly eyes alarm me.